FOR B, MANY YEARS LATER

SIMON & SCHUSTER BOOKS FOR YOUNG READERS

An imprint of Simon & Schuster Children's Publishing Division • 1230 Avenue of the Americas, New York, New York 10020

© 2022 by Daniela Sosa • Book design by Lucy Ruth Cummins © 2022 by Simon & Schuster, Inc.

SIMON & SCHUSTER BOOKS FOR YOUNG READERS and related marks are trademarks of Simon & Schuster, Inc.

For information about special discounts for bulk purchases, please contact

Simon & Schuster Special Sales at 1-866-506-1949 or business@simonandschuster.com.

The Simon & Schuster Speakers Bureau can bring authors to your live event. For more information or to book an event,

contact the Simon & Schuster Speakers Bureau at 1-866-248-3049 or visit our website at www.simonspeakers.com.

The text for this book was set in Futura.

The illustrations for this book were rendered with ink and charcoal pencils and assembled digitally.

Manufactured in China • 0422 SCP • First Edition • 10 9 8 7 6 5 4 3 2 1

Library of Congress Cataloging-in-Publication Data • Names: Sosa, Daniela, author, illustrator. • Title: Friends / Daniela Sosa.

Description: First edition. | New York : Simon & Schuster Books for Young Readers, [2022] | "A Paula Wiseman Book." | Audience:

Ages 4–8. | Audience: Grades K–1. | Summary: A picture book that celebrates friendship—new friends, old friends, friends for a little

while and friends for a lifetime. • Identifiers: LCCN 2021047308 (print) | LCCN 2021047309 (ebook) |

ISBN 9781665911474 (hardcover) | ISBN 9781665911481 (ebook) • Subjects: LCSH: Friendship—Juvenile fiction. | Picture books

for children. | CYAC: Friendship—Fiction. | LCGFT: Picture books. • Classification: LCC PZ7.1.S795 Fr 2022 (print) | LCC PZ7.1.S795

(ebook) | DDC [E]—dc23 • LC record available at https://lccn.loc.gov/2021047308

LC ebook record available at https://lccn.loc.gov/2021047309

FRIENDS

DANIELA SOSA

A Paula Wiseman Book
Simon & Schuster Books for Young Readers
New York   London   Toronto   Sydney   New Delhi

You will meet many
friends, and each
friendship will be different.

Some friends
are there from
the start.

Others come
exactly when
you need them.

Some friendships last only a few moments.

Others last a lifetime.

Friends can be very close

or far away.

Some friendships
don't need words.

Others begin with words

or end with words.

Some friendships grow from a common interest

or are tested by a new arrival.

Some friends can only be seen by you.

Some friendships could have been, but weren't.

Sometimes one

becomes two

becomes three

becomes one again.

There are old friends,

new friends,

best friends,

new best friends.

Some friends will teach you

how to make a
dandelion crown,

how to fix a mistake,

how to whistle,

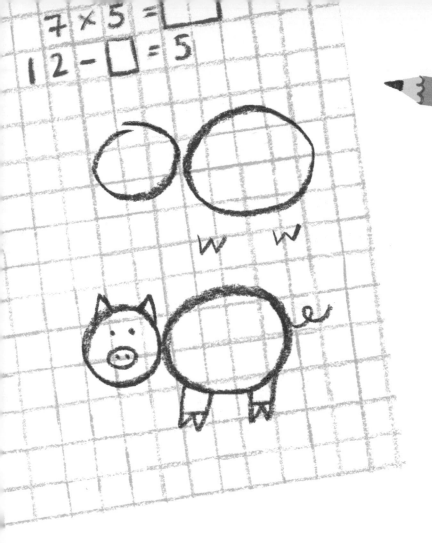

how to draw a
pig from just two circles
and two Ws,

and how to split a lollipop into four.

Friends can
make you brave

or angry

or jealous,

but most important,
they will make you
roll with laughter.

Sometimes you may feel that
you'll never find a friend.

Look closer.